The
Christmas
Letters

The Christmas Letters

A TIMELESS STORY FOR
EVERY GENERATION

BRET NICHOLAUS

CENTER
STREET.

NEW YORK BOSTON NASHVILLE

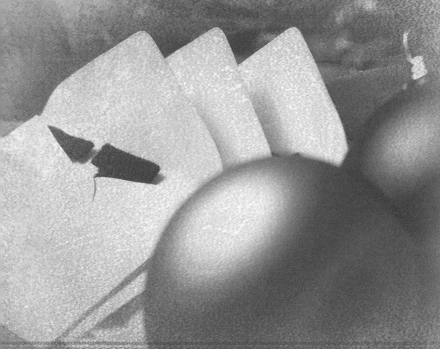

The Christmas Letters

Center Street Edition
Copyright © 2000, 2006 by Bret Nicholaus

This edition is published in arrangement with
Questmarc/William Randall Publishing, P.O. Box 340, Yankton, SD 57078.

Center Street
Hachette Book Group USA
1271 Avenue of Americas
New York, NY 10020

Visit our Web site at www.centerstreet.com.

Center Street® is a division of Hachette Book Group USA.
The Center Street name and logo are trademarks of Hachette Book Group USA.

Printed in the United States of America

First Center Street Edition: October 2006

10 9 8 7 6 5 4 3 2 1

Design by Koechel Peterson and Associates, Inc, Minneapolis, Minnesota

Library of Congress Cataloging-in-Publication Data

ISBN 1-931722-95-1
LCCN 2006926483

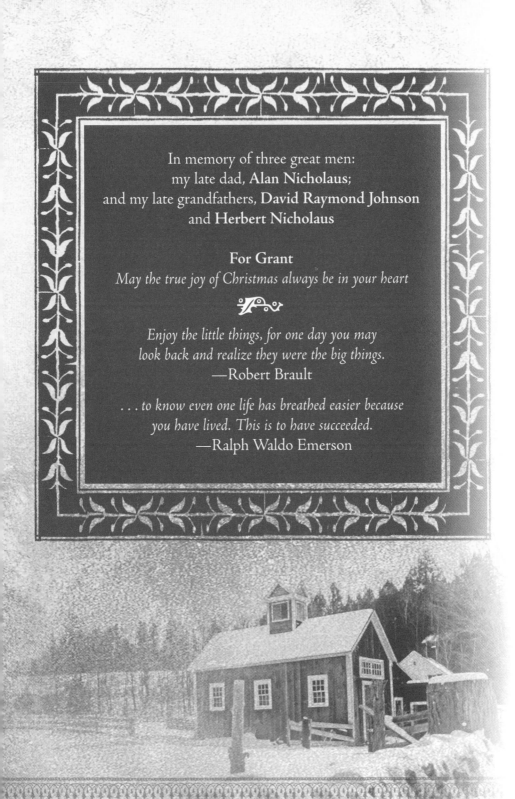

In memory of three great men:
my late dad, **Alan Nicholaus**;
and my late grandfathers, **David Raymond Johnson**
and **Herbert Nicholaus**

For Grant
May the true joy of Christmas always be in your heart

*Enjoy the little things, for one day you may
look back and realize they were the big things.*
—Robert Brault

*. . . to know even one life has breathed easier because
you have lived. This is to have succeeded.*
—Ralph Waldo Emerson

It's been about six months since that cool and rainy June afternoon when Grandpa passed away. Last Christmas Eve, he predicted that he would not be around to celebrate another Christmas with us, but of course we chose not to believe it. As was often the case in our family, we were wrong and Grandpa was right.

THE FIRST FEW MONTHS WITHOUT GRANDPA were hard

for many of us, as the long summer seemed to fade ever so

slowly into fall. But fall, in traditional fashion, picked up the

pace and quickly changed to winter, bringing with it five

inches of snow last Saturday afternoon. Inspired by the beauty

of December's first white blanket, my wife, our six-year-old

daughter, and I spent the evening bringing all our boxes of

holiday decorations down from the attic.

IN THE PAST, PREPARING FOR CHRISTMAS in our

household was more likely to produce a few good arguments

than it was to create feelings of goodwill. The commotion of

Christmas came early and often, and bright spirits rarely

lasted past the first batch of cookies.

*T*HIS YEAR, HOWEVER, THINGS APPEAR to be headed in a different direction. The disagreements, fussing, and overall busyness that usually accompany the month of December are, by and large, absent; sincere joy and a true sense of peace seem to be present in our lives. There is no doubt in my mind that Christmas—and dare I say life in general—has taken on a new meaning, not only for the three of us here but for other members of our family as well.

*A*s I OPENED THE LID ON THE FIRST BOX we carried down from the attic the other night, the very first thing that my fingers grabbed was an off-white envelope containing the Christmas letter Grandpa had given to me last year. For a few brief seconds I stared at the envelope, acutely aware of the fact that the letter was here but Grandpa was not.

I GATHERED MYSELF AND SLOWLY OPENED

the envelope, pulling out the letter, now nearly a year old.

As I did this, I looked down at the box and saw something

else—an old metal train that I put at the base of the

Christmas tree every year. At once, tears welled up in my

eyes and a feeling of loss began to consume me.

You see, the train and the letter were—

well, I suppose that I should take you back a year, to

Christmas Eve, and explain exactly what happened on that

very special night. . . .

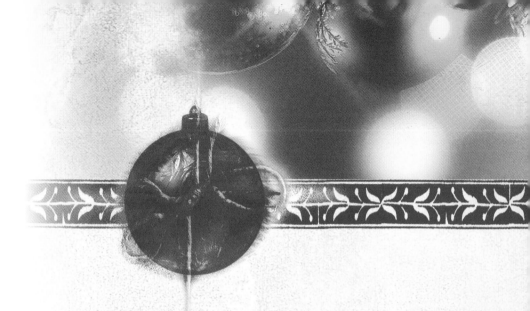

$\mathcal{W}$E WERE CELEBRATING CHRISTMAS at my parents' house, the aroma of simmering spices filling the air and the sumptuous dinner only minutes away from making its grand appearance on the holiday table. For the ten members of our family, it was a typical Christmas Eve.

Conversations ranged from talk about the new home my aunt and uncle had purchased to my dad's new membership in the local country club. I was just beginning to explain why my career had become so demanding of my time when Grandpa, uncharacteristically, interrupted.

"*I* HAVE SOMETHING FOR EACH OF YOU," he said, his

weakened voice sounding momentarily stronger. "I'd like to

hand them out now while we're all seated together." He called

to my mom in the kitchen and beckoned her to take her place

at the table. The roast had about ten minutes to go, so she

came and sat down.

"What's going on, Charles?" inquired my grandma, his wife

of sixty-four years.

Grandpa let out a deep sigh. "As you all know, I'll be eighty-six

next month, and I'm not feeling any better as my days

progress. This may very well be the last Christmas I get to

spend with all of you, so I want to give each of you a personal letter from me." He began to distribute nine sealed envelopes, one to each family member seated at the table.

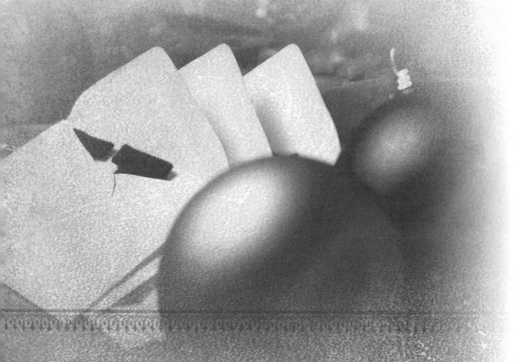

"WHAT'S THE LETTER ABOUT?" asked my wife. She, like the rest of us, was a bit confused by what he was doing.

"I'd like each of you to open it up right now, in front of me. I'd really like that," Grandpa said. He paused briefly before continuing. "John, why don't you start?"

$\mathcal{M}$Y DAD LOOKED AT HIM FOR A FEW SECONDS

and then slowly tore into the envelope with his finger.

He looked inside, obviously perplexed, and pulled out a

letter—a hand-cut, red velvet letter—the letter A.

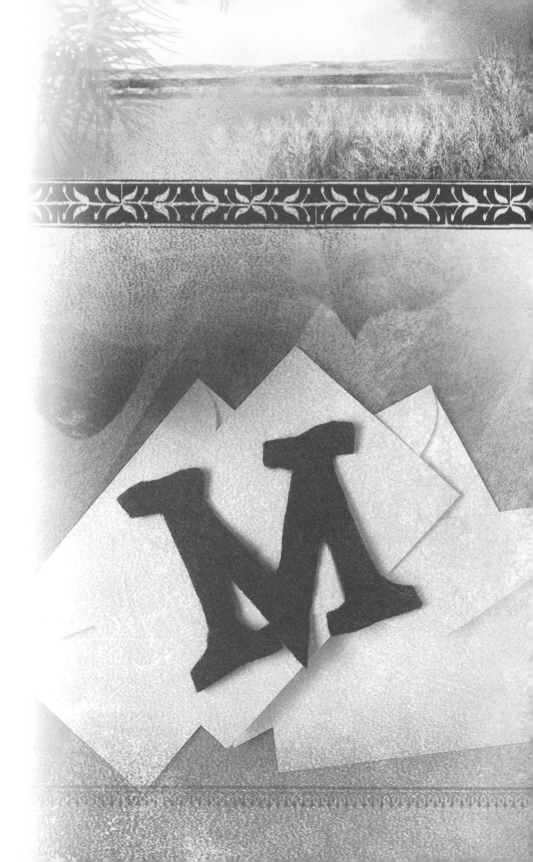

"*I* DON'T GET IT," Dad said very matter-of-factly.

Without providing an answer, Grandpa told my sister, seated next to my dad, to open her envelope. She looked around at all of us and pulled out a red velvet letter M. She and my dad both looked at each other now, but neither knew what to say.

Grandpa motioned to each and every family member sitting at the table. When it was Grandma's turn, she pulled out the letter H; soon the letters R, I, and two S's appeared.

"You're next," Grandpa said as he nodded toward my wife. She opened her envelope and pulled out the letter C.

I was the last one to go. I eagerly opened my envelope to reveal the letter T.

Grandpa sat at the table smiling and looking around at us as if we should have understood what was going on. Unfortunately, we didn't, and finally my sister spoke what was on all of our minds.

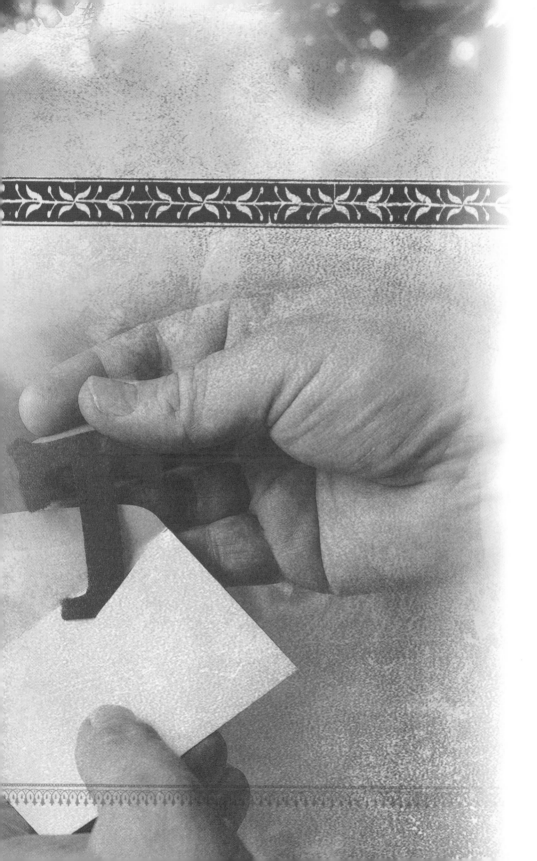

"GRANDPA, THE LETTERS ARE BEAUTIFUL, but what are
they for?"

At this, his facial expression and voice inflection changed. He
was glad that she had asked; in truth, he really hadn't expected
any of us to know what this was all about. Leaning slightly
forward in his chair, he spoke softly but with authority.

"Each one of you is such an important piece

of Christmas to me, and I want you to always remember

that. The letters that you have spell out the word

C-H-R-I-S-T-M-A-S. Take any one of the letters away,

and C-H-R-I-S-T-M-A-S, for me, would not be complete."

It was as if someone had turned the lights on in our heads. We suddenly understood: Each of us was an integral part of Christmas to Grandpa, and he wanted us to have these letters so we would always remember that after he was gone. He had even punched holes in the top of each letter so they could be hung as ornaments on a Christmas tree.

But we soon came to find out that there was much more to these letters than any of us knew.

Proceeding in the order of the letters as they spelled out C-H-R-I-S-T-M-A-S, Grandpa spoke to each person, beginning with my wife.

"Susan, I gave you the letter C. Do you have any idea why?"

After a brief hesitation, she reluctantly admitted that she didn't.

"The letter C stands for Cookies—*your* cookies. Every year, just like this one, you bake a batch of my favorite anise cookies and put them out on Christmas Eve. We both know that nobody else in this family likes them or eats them except for me, yet you bake them anyhow. The fact that you make those cookies just for me—year after year—means more to me than you'll ever know."

A gentle smile crept across my wife's face. What she deemed as a very simple task was obviously incredibly meaningful to Grandpa. He turned next to my grandma.

"SWEETHEART," HE SAID WITH A TWINKLE in his eye,
"the H is for Horse-drawn sleigh. As you well remember,
it was sixty-five years ago tonight that you first told me
that you loved me, while we were out for a sleigh ride
together on your father's farm. That was the first of sixty-five
unforgettable Christmases with you, and every year at this
time, my mind takes me back to that horse-drawn sleigh
ride on that crisp, starry night."

Grandma leaned over, clasped his hand tightly, and gave
him a kiss. She, too, cherished the memory of that night
so many, many years ago.

"SPEAKING OF DAYS GONE BY, the R stands for reminiscing—specifically, your willingness to let me do it," Grandpa said as he looked at his son-in-law holding that very letter. "From the first day I met you, you've always expressed an interest in my stories, especially about what things were like when I was growing up and discovering life.

Very few people I know will listen to those stories, and fewer
still actually inquire about them. But you, you've always
asked . . . and it never means more to me than at Christmas,
when so many wonderful memories drift back from the past.
Whether or not you truly care about what I have to say
doesn't matter; it's the fact that you willingly take the time
to let me share my life's experiences."

My uncle smiled across the table. I, for one, knew that his
ongoing interest in Grandpa's stories was sincere. On many
occasions he had even encouraged Grandpa to write down
the stories for the sake of posterity, but Grandpa had never
followed through on it.

$\mathcal{T}$URNING TO OUR YOUNG DAUGHTER, his only

great-grandchild, he said, "The letter I that you have is for

Imagination—something that you possess so abundantly, and

something that I wish we all had more of. To an old man of

nearly eighty-six years, your imagination is more refreshing

than any words could ever describe. What I wouldn't give

to see life through the eyes of a child again, especially at

Christmas . . . what an incredibly magical time of the year!

I hope that you never lose that childlike wonderment—

and always remember how much it meant to me."

"What does *imagination* mean?" our daughter inquired. All of

us around the table chuckled at the innocence of her question.

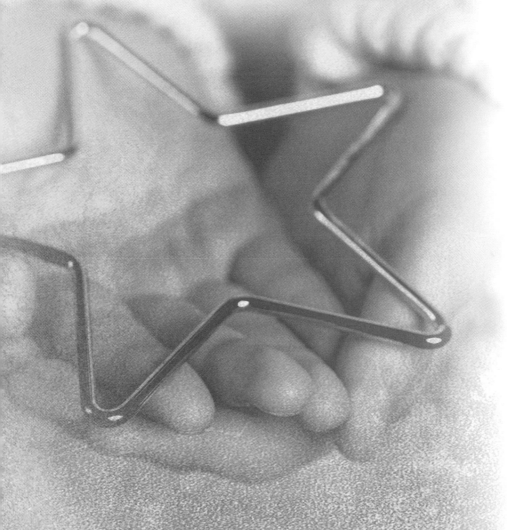

*A*DDRESSING HIS OWN DAUGHTER, he explained why the letter S belonged to her. "The S is for Solo," he said.

Every year since she was sixteen, my aunt has sung a solo at the midnight service at church on Christmas Eve. Grandpa explained that each year her beautiful voice would bring tears to his eyes as he sat with Grandma in the back of the balcony and listened to her sing. Grandpa—a man who rarely verbalized his deepest feelings for his children—had never shared this with her before, and I could tell that my aunt was overcome with happiness.

I held the T and I was next.

"The T is for Train," he said to me. The word was not even out of his mouth when it struck me: Every year, under our Christmas tree, I place an old metal train on some rusty tracks—Grandpa's train from when he was a young boy. He was the son of immigrant parents, and it was the first real Christmas gift his dad had been able to buy for him. Grandpa had given the train to my dad when he turned six years old, and my dad had given it to me when I reached the same age. Knowing that someone still cared about that train—still placed under a tree after eight decades—was so significant to him.

Yet I had never given any serious thought to its emotional value; for me, it had simply been something to fill space under the bottom row of pine boughs.

Whether or not he meant to do it, Grandpa was delivering a lesson worth remembering: It's the little things in life that often mean the most.

Looking at my twenty-eight-year-old sister, he said, "M is for Mistletoe—yes, mistletoe. It's no secret that nobody wants to go out of their way to give a kiss to a wrinkled, elderly man—I sure wouldn't if I were you! And yet you do it every single year. You catch me standing under that mistletoe hanging in the archway of the front door, and then you always run over to give Grandpa a Christmas kiss on the cheek. I love you so much for that."

My sister had that mixed look of being both slightly embarrassed and highly flattered at the same time.

*M*Y DAD HAD THE A. I was pretty certain that I knew what his letter stood for, but I held back the urge to speak my thoughts. The stage that night belonged to Grandpa.

"The A is for Angel. Even after all these years and the fact that you've got a wonderful family of your own, you still let me put the angel in place at the top of your tree. Remember the year that mom and I couldn't be there for the tree-trimming party? You kept the angel off the top until two nights later, when we could finally get to your house. Your willingness to let me have an important part in that annual event is something that has always meant a lot to me."

"It has always meant a lot to us, too," my dad answered.
"It just wouldn't be the same if you didn't top-off the tree."

$\mathcal{T}$URNING TO MY MOM, his daughter-in-law and hostess for the night, he completed the explanation of the letters.

"This S is for Spices . . . the ones that you simmer on the stove every Christmas Eve. It's funny how certain scents bring back such wonderful memories and how they can almost transport you to another time and place. When I was a child, my mother used to simmer cloves and cinnamon on the stove during the holidays. My parents could never afford much of anything, so at an early age I learned to savor even the smallest of pleasures; one of them was Mother's Christmas spices. Every year when I smell that in your house, you take me back to her kitchen during the holidays. I'm very grateful to you for that."

My mom beamed from ear to ear. Until that moment, she never knew that the smell of those spices was so meaningful to Grandpa. Unintentionally, she had been giving him a gift that he treasured year after year.

GRANDPA LEANED BACK IN HIS CHAIR, breathed a deep sigh, and repeated what he had said just minutes before.

"Pull those letters out every year and remember the important piece of Christmas that each of you meant to me."

My aunt got up from her chair and began walking over to give Grandpa a hug. Suddenly, he reached for one more unopened envelope, hidden on his lap.

"I HAVE ONE MORE PIECE OF CHRISTMAS that I'd like to share with all of you," he said.

My aunt stopped in her tracks and then slowly moved back toward her seat, no doubt curious about what he would do next. As he opened the final envelope, a look of incredible resolve came over Grandpa's face. It was as if he wanted us to believe that this was the most important envelope any of us would ever see opened; in many ways, it was.

As each of us fixed our eyes on Grandpa, wondering what this last letter was going to be, my mom spoke up.

"What letter are you going to show us, Dad? All the letters that represent C-H-R-I-S-T-M-A-S have already been handed out."

He reached in and with a slightly trembling hand pulled out one last letter, larger than the others. It was the letter J.

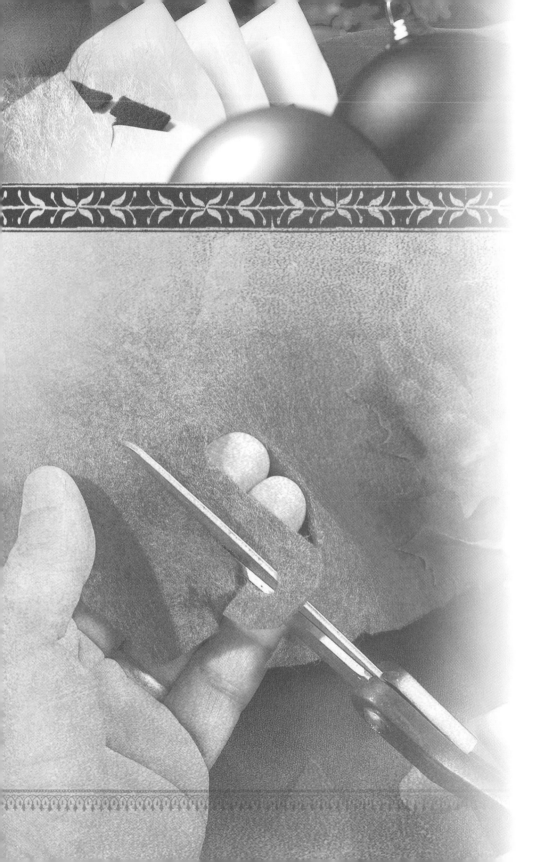

BY THIS POINT IN THE EVENING, I was getting pretty good at guessing what each letter represented. A couple of thoughts raced quickly through my head. J? Maybe it stood for Jingle Bells, but that didn't seem to be worth its own special envelope. Then it hit me: Santa hadn't been mentioned yet in the course of the discussion. Creative as Grandpa was, the J might stand for Jolly Old Saint Nick. What would Christmas be without him? That *had* to be it!

A FEW SECONDS SEEMED LIKE LONG MINUTES as we anxiously awaited the explanation. Then Grandpa spoke: "Without this letter, all the other important pieces of Christmas wouldn't mean nearly as much—not to me, and I hope not to you either. The letter J is for Jesus."

Like everyone else seated at the table, I was stunned at his response. We waited to hear more.

"I know that I've never been an overtly religious man," Grandpa declared. "But I want all of you to know that in my heart, this letter J—what it stands for—is the most important of all."

$\mathcal{W}$E WERE STILL RECOVERING FROM his unexpected response when he raised up the letter in front of his face so that all of us could have a clear look at it. And then he said something that I'll never forget.

"You see," Grandpa said, "without this piece of Christmas, there can be no *peace* of Christmas."

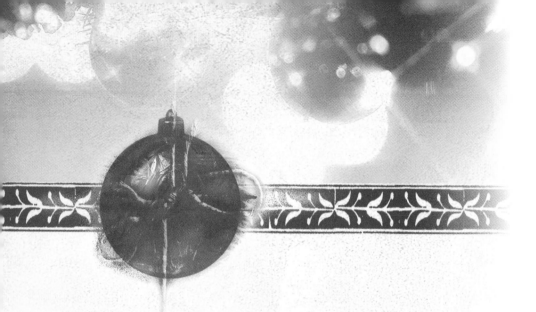

ALTHOUGH THE STATEMENT SEEMED simple enough on the surface, I heard—and felt—in those words something profound. All of a sudden, things like lakeside summer homes, country club memberships, and burgeoning careers appeared insignificant. Perhaps most importantly, it was immediately clear that in the incredibly hectic and stressful pace of the holiday season—with its overcrowded malls, maxed-out credit cards, and endless parties—we had completely lost our focus.

$\mathcal{T}$wo weeks earlier, my wife and I had stood out in the cold and bickered for nearly thirty minutes over whether to buy a Scotch pine or a balsam fir as our Christmas tree. After what had just been said, arguing over a tree seemed not only petty but downright pathetic. It was as if Grandpa had single-handedly put the entire season in its proper perspective, a perspective all too often underappreciated or overlooked altogether.

GRANDPA ASKED MY MOM FOR A PAIR OF SCISSORS.
When he had them in his hand, he took the letter J and
carefully cut it up into ten equal parts. He kept one piece for
himself before handing out the remaining nine, one to each
person at the table.

"The other letters will remind you of what you meant to *my*
Christmas, but I hope that this letter will always remind you of
what Jesus can mean to *your* Christmas," Grandpa concluded.

We sat in a rare moment of quiet and reflection, the smell
of simmering spices wafting our way and the sound of
"Silent Night" playing softly on the kitchen radio....

THE OTHER EVENING, AFTER I HAD PULLED out the

red velvet letter T that Grandpa gave me nearly a year ago,

I thought about that train like never before: how much it had

meant to him and how much more it now means to me. As I

was connecting the last two pieces of track and feeling the

pain of Grandpa's absence, I reached for the wallet in the back

pocket of my pants and pulled out my piece of the letter J.

To someone else, it would look like any other one-inch scrap of hand-cut red velvet; to me, it will always symbolize something infinitely greater. I squeezed it in my hand and pondered its meaning, all the while recalling Grandpa's words: "Without this piece of Christmas, there can be no *peace* of Christmas."

I LOOKED UP TOWARD THE CEILING, but my thoughts reached all the way to heaven. I was no longer sad, but glad.

"Thank you, Grandpa," was all that I could say.

May the peace of God, which passes all understanding, keep your

hearts and minds in Christ Jesus.

—Traditional Apostolic Blessing, based on Philippians 4:7